Pick
Your Own
Quest

Series by Connor Hoover

Wizards of Tomorrow
Alien Treasure Hunters
Pick Your Own Quest

Pick Your Own Quest Books

Pick Your Own Quest: King Tut's Adventure
Pick Your Own Quest: Escape From Minecraft
Pick Your Own Quest: Return to Minecraft
Pick Your Own Quest: Minecraft The End
Pick Your Own Quest: Trapped in A Fairy Tale
Pick Your Own Quest: Dragon vs. Unicorn

DRAGON

vs.

Unicorn

by

Connor Hoover

ROOTS IN MYTH, AUSTIN, TX

Pick Your Own Quest: Dragon vs. Unicorn

A Root in Myth Book
Austin, Texas
For more information, write
connor@connorhoover.com

www.connorhoover.com

Paperback ISBN: 978-1-949717-12-9

For Avalon for being sparkly and
awesome just like Unicorn

Hey there, Dragon and Unicorn lovers! It's me, the author. Just a few quick things I want to tell you before we get this party started . . .

* Don't read this book like other books. If you read this book from beginning to end, it's not going to make sense. You need to follow the instructions at the end of each page. If it tells you to turn to a certain page, then turn to that page (there are page numbers at the bottom of each page)! It's pretty easy. But I just want to be clear. Turn to the page the book tells you to turn to. Got it? Great!

* There are over thirty challenges and over twenty-five endings. When you get to one ending, come right back here and start over. Try to get all the different endings. Try to do all the challenges.

* Oh, and in case you were worried, Dragon and Unicorn end up (sometimes) being friends at the end of the book, even though they might play some tricks on each other throughout.

Okay, that's it. Now let's get this party started!

Turn the page.

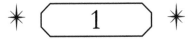

Shown above: Species Dragon. Fierce and mighty. Kind of scary. Approach with caution (or not at all).

Shown above: Species Unicorn. Sparkly and Shiny. Always happy. Approach always.

"Everyone knows that Dragons are the best at everything," Dragon says.

"Not true," Unicorn says. "Everyone knows Unicorns are the best at everything. It's a proven fact."

Dragon is not convinced.

Unicorn is not convinced.

And so the challenge begins.

If you want to be Dragon, turn to page 4.

If you want to be Unicorn, turn to page 6.

Great! You are Dragon, mighty and strong. You are a legend. People fear you from all over the land. There are stories of the epic destruction you cause. Tales about you have been passed down through the ages (since you live so long). But wait! You need a name. A **DRAGON** name.

A good dragon name sounds fierce and also shows your personality. An excellent formula to use for a dragon name is:

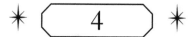

**(something) the (something) of (something)
and the (something) of (something)**

Oh, wait, is that confusing? Here's an example.

RAZZLEHOFF THE DESTROYER OF TEMPLES AND THE COLLECTOR OF KITTENS

What? You don't think "kittens" sounds fierce? Fine. How about this?

BORMICON THE SLAYER OF DEMONS AND THE PLAYER OF VIDEO GAMES

Not any better? Fine. You try.

Write your dragon name (use pencil so you can change it!): _____

_____

_____

Great name! Okay, now turn to page 8.

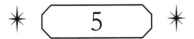

UNICORN

ay to go! You are Unicorn, magical, shiny, and full of happy-making awesomeness! People love you and draw pictures of you (always with rainbows! You love rainbows!). They sing cute little songs about you and tell stories about all the wonderful, magical things you can do. It makes you happy. You are always happy! And you can't wait for Dragon to see how wonderful you are. But you need a name. An awesome, sparkly Unicorn name! A good unicorn name sounds magical and happy. A great formula to use for a unicorn name is:

(happy adjective) (optional happy adjective) (happy noun)

Oh, right. An *adjective* is one of those words that describes things, like *fuzzy* and *dreamy*. And *optional* means you don't have to have it. So if one adjective is perfect, then it's perfect. If two adjectives are perfect, then they're perfect. Here's an example.

Shiny Fluffy Hooves

Cute, right? Or here's another one:

Precious Cupcakes

Oh, that makes me want cupcakes! Now you try.

Write your unicorn name (use pencil so you can change it!): _____

_____

_____

I love that name! Okay, now turn to page 12.

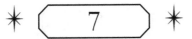

There you are in the park minding your own business, scaring little kids and their parents, when this snooty little unicorn prances up. Her horn looks like it is made of pure gold. Her hair is clean and white and . . . sparkles! How is that even possible? And her mane is colored like a rainbow. She tosses her head around and rainbow glitter flies everywhere. It gets all over the grass, the swings, and you!

"Oh, hi, Dragon," Unicorn says. She doesn't even look at you when she talks. "You should probably leave because I'm about to show all these kids how amazing I am."

"Amazing at what?" you ask. She may toss glitter around like candy, but she can't be all that.

"At everything," Unicorn says.

You laugh and a huge fireball comes out of your mouth. It hits the ground, but a couple sparks bounce back up and almost get in Unicorn's fancy hair.

"Oops, sorry," you say. You're not really sorry. You were here first, so you don't really think you should have to leave.

"What are you laughing at?" Unicorn asks after she makes sure her mane is not on fire.

"You aren't amazing at everything," you say. "In fact, I bet you that I am better than you at pretty much everything."

"Doubt," Unicorn says, and she stands on her back legs and puts her front legs on her sides like she's putting her hands on her hips.

"It's true," you say. "I'm the best."

"At what?" Unicorn says.

You think quick, but nothing comes to mind. "At everything," you say, which is kind of a lame answer, but all you really want is Unicorn to leave so you can go back to scaring kids at the park.

"You are not," Unicorn says.

"Do you want to bet?" you ask.

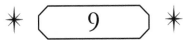

"It won't even be a contest," Unicorn says.

And so the challenge is on. You and Unicorn agree to have a contest to see who is the best.

"Wait here," you say. You are totally ready to show Unicorn that you are better at everything. You fly to your cave super quick and grab the huge spinning wheel you got from the carnival you destroyed last fall. It's exactly what you need for the contest. Now you're ready.

Unicorn is prancing around the park when you get back. All the little kids are clapping. This is not off to a good start.

You show Unicorn the spinning wheel. "This is my Great and Powerful Spinning Wheel," you say. And you explain how you got it at the carnival last fall. You leave out the part about how you destroyed the carnival. Then you give the wheel a spin.

It goes around and around. All the colors blur together like emeralds and rubies. So pretty. You can't take your eyes off it. It slows down and finally stops on one of the choices.

WEIGHT LIFTING

"Weight lifting!" Unicorn says, smoothing out her mane. "What kind of contest is that?"

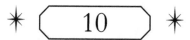

You flex the muscles in your strong arms a few times. "It's a contest that I'm going to win." Everyone knows that dragons are super strong. Even Unicorn has to know that!

You and Unicorn head to the gym.

"Watch this!" you say, and you grab a really heavy bar loaded down with weights. It's not the most you can lift, because you want to save some of your strength for whatever's next. You drop the weight to the ground. The whole gym shakes! Unicorn is never going to be able to do that.

"Oh, is that all there is to it?" Unicorn says. Then she points her horn at the weight bar and magic pours from it. The weight lifts off the ground all by itself!

Magic? You can't believe it! You forgot that unicorns were magic. But you can't let her know you forgot. She might use her magic against you. Still, you need to win this contest.

If you call for best two out of three, turn to page 16.

If you try a new strategy, turn to page 22.

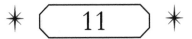

11

Y ou leave your castle for the morning and prance up to the park. The sun is shining. The birds are singing. The flowers are blooming. It's a perfect kind of day! You get to the park and start playing with all the little kids. They love you, and you love them, too. Everyone is happy (making people happy is your superpower). You're about to make a glitter explosion and cover the entire soccer field when a shadow falls over the grass.

You look up to see the meanest looking dragon in the universe here at your park. The kids scream and run away, leaving you there alone with Dragon.

"Go home," you say. "You're scaring everyone." You've always heard that dragons are kind of mean, and this just proves it.

But Dragon plops down on the soccer field instead. The entire ground shakes. "I was only trying to play," Dragon says.

"That's not how you play," you say. You toss your rainbow-colored mane in the air, trying to get glitter on Dragon because maybe that will make him nicer. Glitter makes everything nicer.

He looks really confused. "That is how I play. I think I know how I play."

Oh, this dragon. You say, "What I meant was that there are better ways to play than scaring little kids."

This only makes Dragon more confused. But then a bird flies by, distracting him. He blows a ball of fire at the bird, missing it completely.

"Anyway," you say, trying to get his attention because he seems to have lost focus. "All I'm saying is that maybe you think you're playing, but you're not very good at it."

Dragon starts laughing. He laughs so hard he falls over on his back and kicks his legs up in the air while he laughs.

You scowl at him. You don't like to scowl, but you do want him to stop laughing.

"What's so funny?" you say.

This makes Dragon laugh even harder. "You think you're better than me at playing?"

Of course you are! What a silly statement. "I'm better than you at everything," you say. You don't mean to brag, but you are a unicorn. You are magical. And beautiful. And sparkly.

"No. Way." Dragon says.

And so the challenge is on.

"Let's have a contest," you say. "Wait right here."

You dash back to your castle and collect your magic crystal ball. Then you hurry back to the park.

Dragon is sitting there waiting. At least he hasn't started scaring little kids again.

"This is my magic crystal ball," you say. "It will tell us what to do. Then you'll see that I'm the best at everything."

You try not to sound stuck up, but it comes out a little snooty, even to your ears. You'll have to work on that. But first, the contest.

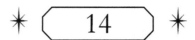

✳ 14 ✳

You look into the crystal ball. Smoke swirls around inside it and then settles.

Throw A Party

You clap your front hooves together. "Oh, I love parties! I will throw the perfect party."

Dragon flaps his giant wings, making your glitter fly everywhere. "What kind of party are we talking about here?" he asks.

Oh no. That's not a good sign. What if Dragon is really good at throwing parties, too? You're going to have to make sure your party is extra special good. You're pretty good at throwing birthday parties, but maybe a summer fun party would be better.

If you throw a summer fun party, turn to page 24.

If you throw a birthday party, turn to page 18.

"Best two out of three," you say.

Unicorn uses her magic to lower the weight bar, and you add more weight and lift it. She does the same . . . with magic. Oh no. That is two times so far that she's done as good as you. If you are going to win this contest, you need to go all in.

You load every weight you can on the bar, but it's not enough. Unicorn could still lift you. So you grab a second weight bar and load it up. It's still not enough. You find a third bar, and after you put a bunch of weights on it, you lift all three bars, one with each of your hands and one with your tail. But your balance is off, and you fall over onto your back.

"Ooof!" you say.

Unicorn comes over and uses magic to lift two of the bars off your chest where they've fallen. She holds them both up at the same time.

"Guess this means I win," she says.

Winner of this round: <u>UNICORN</u>

Overall score: <u>DRAGON 0 – UNICORN 1</u>

Since you've been declared the loser (oh, it hurt to even think that), you spin the wheel for the next challenge.

BIKE RIDING

You almost complain that you're too heavy to sit on a bicycle, but if you do that, Unicorn is going to declare herself the winner or something like that. So instead, you and Unicorn go back to the park where a bunch of bikes are parked in the rack.

Unicorn asks some little kid if she can ride his bike. She sparkles and prances around, and of course the kid says yes. Then Unicorn gets on the bike and rides a perfect circle around the park. She even stays on the sidewalk!

When she gets back to where you're standing, she pushes the bike your way. You hold it by the handlebars as you think about your options. It's way too small for you. But it's not like there are bigger bikes around. You're too big for all of them.

If you try to ride the bike, turn to page 32.

If you look for a bigger bike, turn to page 38.

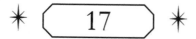

A birthday party is the way to go. Everyone knows what birthday parties are like, and that way Dragon won't do some crazy fun creative summer fun party thing that you never thought of.

"Birthday party!" you say, and you dash off to your castle to get supplies. You collect plates and party hats and you get some streamers. Then you grab even more streamers. Streamers make every party perfect.

Back at the park, you hang the streamers. You get candles. You even find someone to do face painting and balloon animals (but not a clown because sometimes they are scary). You are going to win this contest. When you party is finally set up, you look around for Dragon.

He's just walking up, and with him are two little kids who look like they might be twins.

"Here's my party!" you say, and you dance around and toss your mane and show them the amazing setup you have for the party.

"Nice," Dragon says. "But whose birthday party is it?"

Whose birthday? "Umm . . . I don't know," you admit.

Dragon grins. It's a huge grin, and all his teeth show. "It's not a birthday party if you don't have anyone who's having a birthday."

You don't want to admit it, but he has a really good point.

He pushes the twins forward. "It's their birthday today. Happy birthday!"

The twins hug Dragon and run off to play at the party. Other kids hurry over, and they're all having so much fun, and you know they couldn't be having this much fun if the twins weren't the ones having the birthday. You should have gone with a summer fun party!

Winner of this round: DRAGON

Overall score: UNICORN 0 – DRAGON 1

You're not off to the best start, but you're just getting warmed up. And you can beat a dragon at anything . . . well, except the birthday party thing.

"What's next?" Dragon says.

You look into the crystal ball. The smoke swirls and clears and there is the next challenge.

Bake a Cake

"We should have had cake at the party!" you say. If you'd made a cake then, you might have won the party challenge. But you can definitely win at baking a cake now. Dragon can't be very good at it.

But what kind of cake should you make? There are so many choices. You could go for a fancy cake or a delicious cake. Both are important, and you aren't sure you have enough time to make a cake that is fancy and delicious.

If you make a fancy cake, turn to page 29.

If you make a delicious cake, turn to page 46.

Suddenly you aren't so sure of yourself. What if Unicorn's magic is really strong and she just likes to pretend her only purpose in life is to look pretty? If you're going to win this contest, you need to try something different.

Unicorn is still using her magic to hold up the bar. You grab her with one hand and lift her up in the air. Then you grab the weight bar with your other hand! It's got to be the most you've ever lifted (because Unicorn is not light!). She's as big as a horse. Maybe bigger. And the best part is that she can use her magic to lift things, but she can't use it to lift herself.

Unicorn balances there for a couple seconds then looks down at you and laughs.

"Okay, fine, you win this round," Unicorn says. "Now put me down!"

You put Unicorn down. You also put the weight down.

> **Winner of this round: DRAGON**
>
> **Overall score: DRAGON 1 – UNICORN 0**

You're so strong because you have the best exercise plan ever. You've thought about becoming a personal trainer and helping people get in shape. You could scare people into listening to you.

22

DRAGON'S EXERCISE PLAN

CHASE PEOPLE WHEN THEY SCREAM AND RUN AWAY FROM YOU.

FLAP YOUR WINGS STRONG ENOUGH TO CREATE A TORNADO.

IF SOMETHING GETS IN YOUR WAY ⟨LIKE A BUILDING⟩ NEVER GO AROUND IT. ALWAYS BREAK RIGHT THROUGH IT.

WHEN YOU SEE A TREE, SNAP IT IN HALF LIKE A TOOTHPICK. SEE HOW FAR YOU CAN THROW THE PIECES. THEN LOOK FOR ANOTHER TREE AND REPEAT.

SLEEP AT LEAST 20 HOURS A NIGHT.

Turn to page 26.

✳ 23 ✳

"Summer fun party!" you say. "Here at the park."

Dragon burps and a ball of fire comes out his mouth. He's so rude. If he burped rainbows that wouldn't be rude.

"Half hour," Dragon says. "That's all we get."

Since when does he get to set the rules? Well you did decide what kind of party it would be, so you figure maybe that is fair.

You get to work. You set up slip-and-slides. You make a bubble blowing station. You hook up some sprinklers. When the parents see how excited their kids are getting, they help, cleaning out the sandbox and making sure everything is perfect.

When the half hour timer goes off, you holler, "Party time!"

You hurry over to Dragon with a party hat. You don't need a party hat since you have a shiny golden horn that you would never want to cover up.

Dragon is sitting in the middle of the sandbox, keeping all the kids out.

"Where's your party?" you ask Dragon. As far as you can tell, he hasn't done anything in the last half hour.

Dragon holds up a single balloon. It's yellow. It's also not much of a party.

> **Winner of this round: UNICORN**
>
> **Overall score: UNICORN 1 – DRAGON 0**

Dragon pops the balloon even though he knows the contest was fair. You would never not be fair. Then he looks into the crystal ball. You peek over his shoulder just to make sure he knows what to look for. Not that you'd tell him what to do or anything like that.

Well, maybe a little.

The smoke settles.

Skateboarding

"Yes!" Dragon says. "Dragons are the best at skateboarding, and of skateboarding dragons, I am the best of those."

Uh oh. This is not off to a good start. You tried skateboarding once, but with four feet it was way harder than it should have been. Or maybe it's just hard all the time.

If you skateboard on two feet, turn to page 34.

If you skateboard on four feet, turn to page 40.

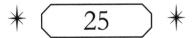

You let Unicorn spin the wheel this time. You already feel pretty good from winning the first round. You try not to watch as it spins round and round so you don't get distracted. If you're going to win this contest, you need to stay focused.

PLAY AT THE PARK

"Play at the park!" Unicorn says when the wheel finishes spinning. "I am the best at playing at the park." She prances around in a circle and swishes her rainbow tail around, making more glitter fly everywhere. You have no idea where the glitter comes from. She must have secret stashes of it hidden away.

You and Unicorn head back to the park. There are at least twenty little kids still around, but their parents pull them out of the way when you get there. They act like you're going to sit on their kids or something. You only sat on a kid one time, and it was totally the kid's fault. Also, he was fine, so no big deal. People always overreact when they see you.

When you normally come to the park, you scare little kids. That's playing for you. You go first and you rush around, stomping really loud and bellowing in your loudest dragon voice. The kids all scream and run, hiding behind park benches and slides. You let a tiny bit of fire escape from your nostrils every so often, but you make sure not to catch the playscape on fire since you don't actually want to hurt anyone. You would definitely lose that way. When you're done, you casually saunter back to Unicorn. She's standing there with her mouth open. A confused look covers her face.

"What did you do?" she says.

"I played." You cross your arms and wait. No way can she do better. You got every single kid at the park to play with you. They loved it! Even now, they're barely peeking their heads back out.

"That's not how I play," Unicorn says. She prances over to the swing set and swings really high. Then she goes down the slide so fast you barely see her. She uses her front legs to cross the monkey bars. Then she climbs on the see-saw.

"Come on, Dragon!" Unicorn says. "We have to do this together. It will be fun!"

You don't see how that's playing but you go over and jump onto the other side of the see-saw. Unicorn flies up high into the air! Rainbows fly from her so she looks like a rainbow shooting star. All the little kids start clapping. No way. You were totally playing better, and she is going to win. She lands on the ground perfectly, like some magical gymnast and bows. Glitter surrounds her in a cloud! The little kids clap even harder. You need to do something or all is lost.

If you try the Merry-Go-Round, turn to page 43.

If you try the spinning thing, turn to page 36.

✳ 28 ✳

You don't know if Dragon can even bake a cake, but what if he can and he's really great at it? After all, lots of mythical creatures like to make cakes . . . don't they? Anyway, a fancy cake is the way to go.

You and Dragon head back to the kitchen at your castle since he doesn't have a kitchen in his dragon cave. You are on one side of the kitchen. He's on the other. You mix the batter and pour it into a pan, and then you collect all your very best decorating things that you've been saving for the perfect occasion. This is definitely that moment.

You ice your cake with pink, blue, and green stripes. You put glitter on the entire thing. You add sprinkles that match the icing. You make flowers and put them around the edges.

You turn around and place it on the counter to show Dragon. He also has a cake. It's not pretty. It's not even iced. But the outside has a perfect golden layer of crust. You start to get a really bad feeling, but you don't know why.

"Nice cake, Unicorn," Dragon says.

"Thank you! And I have candles for us." You place two candles into the cake. They sink down down down until they disappear inside the cake.

Dragon narrows his eyes at the cake. "Did you bake it?"

That's why you have such a bad feeling. You knew you forgot something.

"No," you say. "But it is really pretty." You batt your eyelashes when you say this, hoping it will win you the contest.

It doesn't happen.

Winner of this round: <u>DRAGON</u>

Overall score: <u>UNICORN 0 – DRAGON 2</u>

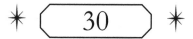

Okay, so the cake thing was a disaster. Raw cakes don't even make you happy. But the competition is not over. You and Dragon look into the crystal ball to see what's next.

Swimming

Whoa. You will be the first to admit that swimming is not what you are best at. You like splashing an awful lot. But actual swimming is different. The water can be so deep, your hair gets all wet, and you aren't even really sure how to do it. But this isn't a splashing contest.

You pretend to act like you're excited. "Oh, where should we swim?"

"How about the ocean?" Dragon says.

The ocean sound horrible. If you don't think fast, you'll be in the middle of deep water with sharks everywhere. You wonder if they will eat you before or after you drown. It's the worst thought you've ever had in your life, and it definitely doesn't make you happy.

If you suggest a pool, turn to page 70.

If you suggest a bathtub, turn to page 50.

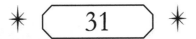

You have never ridden a bike this small, but it might be sturdier than it looks.

"Here I go!" you say, and you get onto the bike.

It is crushed under your massive dragon weight.

Winner of this round: UNICORN

Overall score: DRAGON 0 – UNICORN 2

This is not going well at all. You spin the wheel again, and it's like you've wished on a lucky star and your wish has come true.

TAKE A NAP

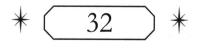

"Yes!" you say. Nobody is better than you at taking a nap. You've taken a nap before for an entire century. One time you slept through a battle that lasted for ten years. You are going to be the best.

"Why would anyone want to take a nap?" Unicorn asks. "There are so many fun things to do!"

Unicorn has way too much energy.

"Two hour nap," you say. "Starting now."

Then you flop over onto your side right there at the park. Just as you're drifting off to sleep, you think that maybe you should set an alarm, just as a backup. You're sure you'll wake up, but this park grass is pretty comfy. Still, your eyes are so tired. You don't want to get back up.

If you get up and set an alarm, turn to page 84.

If you don't worry about an alarm—you'll wake up on time—turn to page 42.

✳ 33 ✳

The last time you tried skateboarding, it must have been so hard since you used all four of your feet. To win this time, you need to stand on your back legs only.

Dragon grabs a skateboard from some kid who immediately starts crying and runs off to tell his mommy. Then Dragon jumps onto the board and zips around the park like some skateboarding expert. In fairness, he did say he was good at skateboarding. Oh well. You can do better.

There's a cute little kid who lets you use his skateboard. Was the board really this small last time? You set one foot on it and it slips out from underneath you. Dragon laughs. You're tempted to use your magic on him and make his scales change to the color of poop, but you don't. That wouldn't be nice.

You try again, holding onto a park bench as you get on. So far so good. You get both feet on the board. Then, in your biggest moment of bravery, you let go of the park bench. You roll for about two feet and then the board wobbles.

You fall off. And you are not getting back on.

> **Winner of this round: <u>DRAGON</u>**
>
> **Overall score: <u>UNICORN 1 – DRAGON 1</u>**

Dragon grabs the crystal ball and looks inside. His eye is almost as big as it. You look around him just as the smoke is settling.

Clean Your Room

Dragon starts laugh. "Why would anyone clean their room?"

Why would anyone *not* clean their room? Having a messy room makes no sense to you. You love organizing anything and everything. This contest will be a breeze.

Dragon insists that there is no way he's cleaning his cave. He likes his gold all over the place. So you, being the wonderful kind unicorn that you are offer up a couple rooms at your castle. You and Dragon head off to the castle. The problem is that all the rooms are neat.

"How about I mess up a room and you clean it, and you mess up a room and I clean it?" Dragon says.

If you each mess up your own rooms, turn to page 54.

If you mess up each other's rooms, turn to page 74.

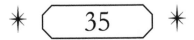

✳ 35 ✳

You can't let Unicorn win! You notice there is one thing she hasn't tried at the park. It's green and spins around in a circle. You dash over to it, and with a running start, you jump on it and hold on. It spins around and around, faster and faster. At first it's kind of fun. You even catch yourself giggling. But then your head starts to feel really funny and dizzy and everything is blurring together. You have to get off the spinning thing.

But it won't slow down! It keeps spinning! This is the worst. Why would anyone ever put one of these at a park, anyway? If you don't get off, you think you might throw up. The thing is spinning a million miles an hour, but you let go anyway. Bad idea.

You fly off it, through the air, and hit hard into the playscape, smashing it into little pieces. You're covered in playground mulch, and you did destroy the playscape, but at least you are free of the spinning thing.

Unicorn prances over to you. Your head is still spinning, and it looks like there are three of her.

"I won," she says.

You do throw up.

Winner of this round: UNICORN

Overall score: DRAGON 1 – UNICORN 1

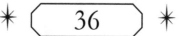

You don't even care that Unicorn won that round. You're just so happy to be off the spinning thing.

Unicorn spins the wheel because you're barely able to stand after the park disaster.

PAINT A PICTURE

Unicorn dances around and claps her hands (well her front hooves) together. "Oh, I love paining! I'll paint a rainbow and flowers and sunshine and birds."

You feel too sick to paint anything that happy.

Unicorn sets up two art easels and hands you a flat thing with a bunch of colors and a tiny little brush.

"What am I supposed to do with this stuff?" you ask.

"Paint with it." Then she starts to paint, using all the bright colors so her picture looks really happy and cheerful.

You aren't feeling very happy and cheerful. You don't feel like sunshine and flowers. But you also don't want to lose the painting contest.

If you paint happy things, turn to page 80.

If you paint how you really feel, turn to page 58.

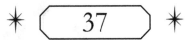

You may not know everything, but you do know one thing. Okay, you know a lot, but let's focus on the bike riding. If you get on this tiny little bike, it is going to smash into itty bitty pieces. You cannot win a competition that way.

You pass the bike back to the little kid. He actually looks really relieved. Did he think you were going to actually ride it? Then you look out to the parking lot, and your mind starts churning.

You pull a couple tires off a car and put them near each other. Then you break off a telephone pole and use it to hold the two tires together. Finally you grab a couple park benches to use as the pedals.

The tires almost don't hold you, but pretty soon you get your balance, and around and around the park you go. You go faster each time, waving at Unicorn as you pass her.

"Hi, Unicorn," you say the first time you pass her.

"Hi, Unicorn," you say again every time.

Her smile is less happy each time you pass.

Finally when you're sure you've won, you pop the front wheel up into a wheelie just to make sure. Then you blow fire out your nostrils to make it look even more awesome. All the little kids clap!

> **Winner of this round: DRAGON**
>
> **Overall score: DRAGON 1 – UNICORN 1**

Unicorn mutters something under her breath about it not technically being a bicycle, but whatever. It's on to the next contest. You spin the wheel.

MAKE SOMETHING OUT OF CLAY

Unicorn sees the challenge and jumps up and down with excitement. "I love art projects!" Unicorn says.

Art projects? Clay isn't for art projects, is it?

Unicorn suggests you go to a local pottery studio because they have the best clay. You've seen pretty good clay down by the river.

If you go to the art studio, turn to page 62.

If you go to the river, turn to page 82.

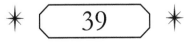

You think about skateboarding on two feet, but . . . you have four feet! There must be a reason for that. And you just have to be you!

The last time you tried skateboarding, the board was really small. What you need is a bigger board.

There are at least ten kids at the park skateboarding, and you sparkle and shine and ask them if you can borrow their skateboards. Of course they agree. Kids love you. Everyone loves you!

Using your unicorn magic, you hold all the boards together. Then you climb on with all four feet and you're off! You ride around the park and you are perfect. This is nothing like last time. You ride through the grass. Through the sand. Even the gravel. A lot of the gravel sprays everywhere on the sidewalk, but that doesn't bother you.

When you're finally done, you stop in front of Dragon.

"Your turn!" you say. Dragon is going to have a hard time beating you.

He scares the kids into letting him use their skateboards also, and then he takes off. But he's not far away when the wheels hit some loose gravel. Dragon goes flying off the skateboards and lands on his bottom.

Winner of this round: UNICORN

Overall score: UNICORN 2 – DRAGON 0

Dragon complains about the course not being clean, but you had a clear victory. You look into the magic crystal ball to see what is next. But what you see is not a contest at all.

Turn to page 48.

While you sleep, you have an amazing dream that you are the king of the world. Aliens with three heads attack and only you can save the world from them. The people love you. They beg you to be their king forever.

DRAGON FOR KING

VOTE DRAGON FOR KING OF THE WORLD!

IF ELECTED, DRAGON PROMISES TO

* PROTECT THE WORLD

* COLLECT ALL THE GOLD AND KEEP IT SAFE AND SECURE

* BURN EVERY BIT OF TRASH

* MAKE DAILY NAPS MANDATORY

* EAT ANY ALIENS WHO ATTACK

It's a good dream. The aliens taste like chicken.

Turn to page 68.

You jump onto the Merry-Go-Round, and you look for one of the horses that will fit you. Maybe the kids will think it's cute and clap for you. But you're too big to sit on any of the horses! This was a bad idea. Except then a little kid walks up and taps you on the end of your tail. You almost swat him away with your tail, but he gives you a smile that's kind of cute and asks if he and his sister can ride on your back on the Merry-Go-Round.

Ride on our back? Doesn't he realize that you are a powerful, scary dragon? Maybe you should tell him your name and see if he is terrified. Ah, whatever. You're

about to lose the contest anyway, so you agree. The kid and his sister scramble up your tail and onto your back. Around and around you go, and when the ride is over, three more kids stand there waiting. You let them all ride. They giggle and smile and pat your head. It makes you feel ridiculous . . . and almost kind of happy.

Finally you can't take the Merry-Go-Round music anymore, so you walk back over to Unicorn, trying not to knock anything over as you go.

"I guess you win this round, too," Unicorn says. She brushes some mulch from her rainbow-colored mane.

"But the kids loved you," you say. They'd clapped so hard for Unicorn. It's hard for you to admit.

"They loved you more," Unicorn says.

Who are you to argue?

Winner of this round: DRAGON

Overall score: DRAGON 2 – UNICORN 0

You spin the wheel. After the Merry-Go-Round, it's easier to watch the spinning wheel. It slows down and finally lands.

HOPSCOTCH

You've never played hopscotch before, but how hard can it be?

Unicorn has some rainbow-colored chalk and draws out the grid to play. Then she tosses a beanbag and hops along gracefully from one number to the next, prancing like she's in a pony show, not an epic contest to see who is better. She grabs the beanbag with her teeth and hops back perfectly.

You start sweating. You're going to have to be perfect if you're going to beat her.

"Not bad," you say. "But watch this." You pick up the beanbag. It smells like real beans and it makes you hungry. But you will not eat the beanbag. You throw it, but it doesn't even land on one of the number squares.

"I think you missed," Unicorn says.

If you tell Unicorn that you didn't miss, that you meant to throw it there, turn to page 52.

If you ask to throw it again, turn to page 72.

A delicious cake is the way to go. As long as it tastes amazing, people will love it.

You and Dragon go to a local cake shop and you ask if you can use their kitchen to bake your cakes. They agree as long as they get to live stream the competition. They say it will be great for business.

"That's a fun idea!" you say, and you get to work. You measure out all your ingredients perfectly, making sure not to put an extra grain of salt in. Too much salt and it will be ruined. Too little sugar and no one will want to eat it. It's a tricky balance, but you can do this.

Then, just before you put it in the oven, you add a little unicorn magic, to make it extra special tasty delicious.

You set a timer, and the second it dings, you take your cake out of the oven. By now tens of thousands of people are watching the live stream, so you make sure to sparkle and toss glitter around also.

The cake store owners try your cake and say it is amazing. Of course it is! It has unicorn magic in it. Then Dragon sets his cake down on the counter.

Half of it is missing.

"I got hungry," Dragon says when you ask where it went. Then he grabs the other half and eats that, too.

Without a cake to taste, you are the clear winner!

Winner of this round: UNICORN

Overall score: UNICORN 1 – DRAGON 1

Sweet! Now you're catching up. A couple more rounds, and Dragon will never be able to claim to be the best.

"Ready for the next challenge?" you ask Dragon.

His face is still covered in frosting. "Yep."

You both look into the crystal ball. The smoke only swirls for a second.

Sing A Song

Well, singing isn't what you're the best at. Your voice is a little hoarse. But you can certainly sing better than Dragon.

You and Dragon go to a Karaoke studio and pay for a room. Dragon is so big that it's pretty cramped in there. There are so many songs to choose from. Maybe you should sing a happy song. Or maybe a sad song. Or maybe a slow song. The choices are endless.

If you sing a fun, happy song, turn to page 56.

If you sing a sad song, turn to page 60.

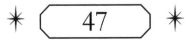

The smoke swirls around in the crystal ball, changing colors. It's so pretty. As you watch it, a vision forms inside.

You're running around a field, playing with other unicorns. They are all your best friends, and you have so much fun together. Then you decide to open an amusement park. You have games and rides and even a cotton candy maker. It's your favorite. You make pink and blue and yellow cotton candy and you eat so much that your tummy hurts. But then you eat more cotton candy, and it stops hurting.

You hang a sign out front of the amusement park.

NO DRAGONS ALLOWED

You and your friends paint rainbows everywhere, and you make magical elves and cute little animals that fly and breathe fire.

Oh wait. That's like Dragon. If no dragons are allowed, you can't make dragons.

The vision disappears, and a new challenge appears.

Grow Flowers

"Grow flowers?" Dragon says. "Why would anyone want to grow flowers?"

You almost tell him how amazing you are at growing flowers, but you aren't sure you can trust Dragon. He might try to steal your flowers and pretend they are his.

"Flowers are kind of pretty," you say. You actually love flowers, and you are so good at growing all sorts of them.

"Rocks are pretty," Dragon says. "We should grow rocks instead."

You giggle because Dragon is so silly. "You can't grow rocks."

"Hmmm . . . ," Dragon says. "Maybe you can't grow rocks. But I can."

Wait a second. This is not how the contest is supposed to go.

"Let's grow rock flowers," Dragon says. "Then we'll both be happy."

You don't think that will make you happy, but you don't see a way to get out of it now. And you are good at growing all kinds of different flowers. Maybe you can grow rock flowers.

If you try to grow rock flowers, turn to page 65.

If you fake growing rock flowers, turn to page 77.

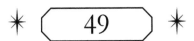

"We should swim in a bathtub," you suggest.

Dragon laughs. "A bathtub! Silly Unicorn!"

Then he grabs you and flies away, to the ocean. Once you're over the water, he drops you.

You fall and scream and scream and fall. "I can't swim!" you shout.

Suddenly something plummets toward you and grabs you before you hit the water.

It's Dragon!

"You saved me!" you shout. "Thank you so much!"

Dragon flies you back to land and sets you down. "This means I am better at swimming," Dragon says.

"Yes, you are!" You could not be more happy to agree about something.

Winner of this round: DRAGON

Overall score: UNICORN 0 – DRAGON 3

You have one last chance to prove to Dragon that you are better than him. But you're also really happy to be alive. You look into the swirling smoke inside the crystal ball.

Dance Contest

Finally! Something you are one hundred perfect better at.

"Let's go to the dance club," you say, and Dragon flies you there. Once you're both inside, you move to the center of the dance floor. The people clear to the edges and clap for you both.

Dragon starts dancing. Well, it's not really dancing. It's more like he's moving all the different parts of his body in jerking motions and sneezing all at the same time.

When he's done, you say, "What kind of dance was that?"

"Modern," Dragon says.

Modern dance? You've never heard of it. But the people are all clapping. You need to be amazing if you want to win.

If you do ballet, turn to page 150.

If you do Hip Hop, turn to page 135.

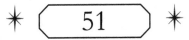

"**I** meant to throw it there," you say.

Unicorn does not look convinced. "What number is that?"

"Infinity," you say. You've heard that infinity is a pretty big number. Then you bend your knees and jump through the air. You jump across the entire hopscotch board without touching a single chalk line and land on one foot. You grab the beanbag with your claws, and then you jump back to where you started.

"Hmmm, I don't think you broke any rules," Unicorn says. "And you did get farther without touching the lines." She almost seems disappointed. But then again, you've been better at everything so far.

"So I win?" you ask. You try to sound like you aren't really excited just so Unicorn doesn't change her mind.

Unicorn rolls her eyes. "Yeah, you win, but we need to set better rules in the future."

Rules! Whatever.

Winner of this round: <u>DRAGON</u>

Overall score: <u>DRAGON 3 – UNICORN 0</u>

Then Unicorn spins the wheel.

FLY

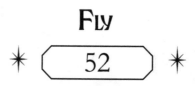

✳ 52 ✳

"Not fair!" Unicorn says when the wheel stops. "I don't have wings."

"But you're magical," you say, trying not to smile. You are totally going to win. "Maybe you can fly and you just don't know it."

"Maybe," Unicorn says, but she looks doubtful.

You are ahead by three. You could make this round a little more fair. Maybe. "How about I don't use my wings?" you say. That seems pretty fair to you.

"You can't fly without wings," Unicorn says.

"Of course I can," you say. You have no idea how, but you'll figure it out. You are a dragon after all, and dragons can fly. Well some dragons can fly. Some can't fly, but you are definitely of the flying kind.

Unicorn goes first. She stands there and looks pretty, tossing her mane around, but she definitely doesn't fly. She jumps up off the ground a few times, but if that's flying, then you'll eat a bicycle.

"Wow, you got way up in the air that time," you say, trying to fake it like you're encouraging her. But even without wings, you can do better than that.

If you try jumping like Unicorn, turn to page 111.

If you try flying without wings, turn to page 136.

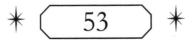

53

"I'll mess up my room and clean it, and you mess up your room and clean it," you say to Dragon.

He grins like this was his plan all along. Then you go into your separate rooms.

You look around the room. Everything is so pretty and perfect, and no matter how hard you try, you can't mess it up. Well, Dragon doesn't have to know that. You wait for a solid fifteen minutes and then you head back out and knock on Dragon's door.

He grumbles something that sounds like, "Come in," so you go inside. The room is a disaster, with everything in a big pile in the center of the room. Dragon is sitting on top of the pile.

"Did you clean at all?" you ask, trying not to worry about how long this will take to fix.

"A little," Dragon says. "Did you mess up at all?"

You think about lying. You really do. But no matter how hard you try, you can't do it.

"No!" you shout. "I couldn't mess up my room!"

> **Winner of this round: DRAGON**
>
> **Overall score: UNICORN 1 – DRAGON 2**

You "help" Dragon clean the room (which is really just you cleaning and Dragon telling you how much gold he has, but whatever), and then you look into the crystal ball again.

Make a Milkshake

Yes! Milkshakes are delicious.

"I'm lactose intolerant," Dragon says.

You don't know what that is or why it matters. "That's okay," you say. Then you and Dragon head to the local ice cream shop and ask if you can have a milkshake making contest.

There are so many flavors to choose from. It's hard to decide which flavor to use in your milkshake. You could use a few different flavors or you could stick with just one.

If you use a few different flavors, turn to page 118.

If you stick with one flavor, turn to page 158.

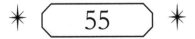

A fun happy song is definitely the way to go. You pick the perfect song from the Karaoke machine and grab the microphone. You hit the low notes just fine, but you totally forgot how many high notes were in this song! You miss them all. Dragon actually covers his ears as you're signing.

"You are so overreacting," you say once you're done.

"Nope," Dragon says. Then he picks a song and starts singing.

He's chosen a sad song. It's about a mountain and people who used to live there and want to go home. You try not to cry. You really do. But before you realize it, tears are leaking out of your eyes. Curse Dragon and his sad song!

Winner of this round: <u>DRAGON</u>

Overall score: <u>UNICORN 1 – DRAGON 2</u>

This is not looking so good for you. You need to make better choices. Happy choices. Choices that will help you win. You look into the crystal ball.

Clean a Toilet

"I love cleaning toilets!" (said no one ever.)

Okay, so cleaning toilets isn't your favorite thing to do, but you are really good at it. You're good at cleaning everything.

"Do people clean toilets?" Dragon says.

You got this contest no problem.

You and Dragon find the grossest toilets you possibly can find. They're outside in some concrete building near a park that no one ever comes to.

Dragon takes one look inside, crosses his arms, and says, "No way am I cleaning in there."

You take a peek also, and OMG it is the worst thing you've ever seen! You could agree with Dragon, and both not clean, or you could say that you have to clean because the crystal ball told you to.

If you agree to not clean the toilets, turn to page 102.

If you insist on cleaning, turn to page 120.

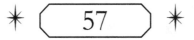

Sunshine and rainbows are not how you feel. If you paint that, it's going to be horrible. Already you aren't feeling so good about this painting thing, but you have to do something. You dig your claw into the paint and start by painting a lonely mountain with dark clouds of red and purple around it. In front of the mountain, you draw a river. But then you get kind of hungry since you threw up your entire lunch, so you draw a town by the river and you make sure there are lots of people in the town. If you lived in that lonely mountain, you would eat all the people. Then you paint flames everywhere.

You step back when you're done. It's pretty epic, if you do say so yourself.

Unicorn looks over your shoulder at the painting. It's not happy like her painting. But she says, "It's so inspired."

"Really?" Maybe she's messing with you.

"Really," Unicorn says. "This is the kind of painting people will talk about forever."

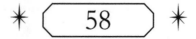

Winner of this round: <u>DRAGON</u>

Overall score: <u>DRAGON 2 – UNICORN 1</u>

You're feeling pretty good after winning the picture painting contest, so you give the wheel a spin.

Do A Math Problem

If you have twenty-four pieces of gold and you get four new pieces of gold every day for thirty days and then you destroy one town, how many pieces of gold do you have?

Oh, this is hard! I mean the part about the gold isn't hard. You count gold all the time. But what about that part with the destroying one town? This could be a trick question.

If you answer and ignore the part about destroying the town, turn to page 159.

If you factor in the gold you would get from the destroyed town, turn to page 104.

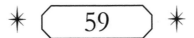

A sad song is the way to go. People care about sad songs and cry over them, and if Dragon cries when you sing your song, you will win.

Dragon insists on going first. He picks some song that sounds like people reciting poetry. He calls it rap. It's not all bad, but there are lots of words in it that you don't think are appropriate to say.

When he's done, you tell him this. He grumbles and almost says some of the bad words again, but you hold up a hoof and say, "Language."

He grumbles some more. Then you start singing.

You sing a song about alligators and geese and how you were supposed to get on some boat when the world flooded but you didn't and you were washed away, and that's why lots of people think unicorns don't exist. It's really sad. When you finish, you wipe tears from your eyes.

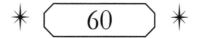

Dragon wipes tears from his eyes, too!

Winner of this round: UNICORN

Overall score: UNICORN 2 – DRAGON 1

Dragon tries to pretend that he wasn't crying, but you know better. You pat him on the arm and tell him that it's okay to show emotion. Then you stop at a local chocolate shop and both have a big piece of chocolate before heading back to the park. Then it's on to the next challenge.

The crystal ball swirls and swirls and finally stops.

Shoot Hoops

"Score!" Dragon says, and he grabs a basketball from some little kid who's trying to dribble it.

You apologize to the kid, but you guys do need a basketball if you're going to shoot hoops.

Dragon shoots first . . . and makes it!

You go . . . and miss.

Oh, no. Time for a new strategy.

If you use unicorn magic, turn to page 140.

If you think using magic isn't fair, turn to page 110.

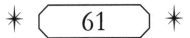

61

You've never been to a pottery studio in your life, but Unicorn seems pretty sure that their clay can be used to make anything, so you agree. When you get there, you can't fit through the door, but the pottery person is really nice and comes outside to bring you a lump of clay.

A very small lump of clay.

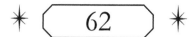

There is no way you can make anything out of this little clay. It's hardly a snack. You aren't even sure it is clay because it's so smooth and there are no rocks or sticks in it. You lick it to be sure.

Yep, it's clay. But it's still too small.

You smash it into the ground because you're kind of frustrated, and then you drag your claws through it.

Oh, wait. That made a cool design. You trace your claws again, this time making lines and little angles like mountains and some tiny things that look like trees. You keep at it, and when you're finished, you blow fire at it until it hardens into a stone. Then you show it to Unicorn.

"You made a cool map," Unicorn says. "I wish I'd thought of that."

You didn't know it was a map, but it makes you sound really worldly to be making maps so you nod. Then Unicorn holds up her creation. It's a vase. On the shelf inside the pottery studio are at least twenty other vases. Hers is good, but it's not that original. Also, it still needs to be fired.

Winner of this round: DRAGON

Overall score: DRAGON 2 – UNICORN 1

Unicorn sets the vase on the shelf with the others and spins the wheel. It goes around a couple times and then lands.

PLAY THE PIANO

What! There is no way you can play a piano with claws.

"What!" Unicorn says. "There is no way I can play a piano with hooves."

Maybe winning won't be hard after all.

There's a church down the road, and it even has a door big enough for you to fit inside. Well, you do break the door frame, but no one is watching. The piano is right up front and it's one of those giant ones so big an elephant could play it (if elephants could play pianos. Maybe they can. Next time you see an elephant, you can ask.).

"Oh, can I go first?" Unicorn says. She waves her mane around so it flows in the air like a rainbow river. Glitter sparkles and lands on the piano keys.

If you let Unicorn go first, turn to page 116.

If you go first, turn to page 100.

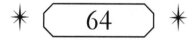

Magical

You and Dragon head over to where there are piles of rocks. You look around for the best place to grow rock flowers, but can't figure it out. There are brown rocks, rough rocks, small rocks. Does it make a difference when growing rock flowers? Ugh! You don't know what to do.

Okay, you can think this through. Rock flowers must grow the same as normal flowers. You find a small, shiny rock and you tuck it under some bigger rocks. Then you fill a watering can and pour it slowly over the rocks. You make sure you aren't casting a shadow on the rock flower because all flowers need sunshine to grow.

You wait a really long time (at least ten minutes). Then you pour some more water on it. It's still not growing. Maybe you need to use magic to help it grow. You focus all the magic from your horn and point it at the rock seed. If this doesn't work, nothing will.

Nothing happens. All you have when the time limit is up is a small pile of wet rocks.

You let out a deep sigh because you've never failed at growing flowers before. You look over to Dragon. He's standing next to a flower growing out of the rocks!

"No way!" you say. This is not possible.

"I don't know," Dragon says. "It sure looks like a rock flower to me."

He must've cheated. But you didn't see him cheat, so you can't call him out on it. But he is not better at growing flowers than you. Luckily you are still ahead.

Winner of this round: <u>DRAGON</u>

Overall score: <u>UNICORN 2 – DRAGON 1</u>

You try your very best to forget about the rock flowers and you look into the crystal ball. The smoke swirls around and settles.

Play Video Games

"Yes!" you and Dragon both shout at the same time.

What? You know you're amazing at playing video games, but how does Dragon play video games? He can't possibly have electricity wired into his cave. Maybe he doesn't know what video games are. Well, that's not your problem.

You and Dragon head to a nearby video arcade. There are a bunch of old-looking games and a lot of newer ones, too.

Dragon saunters up to the one with the most flashing lights and pulls two quarters from his pocket. "High score wins," he says.

Maybe he does know what video games are. Then you notice the list of high scores on the game he picked. They all have the same three letters: **DGN**.

That can't be him! This is already not fair and the game hasn't even started yet. If you play his favorite video game, you will never win. If you don't, he'll think you're backing down. And unicorns never back down from anything.

If you play Dragon's favorite game, turn to page 95.

If you suggest a different game, turn to page 112.

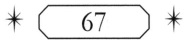

Y ou don't need an alarm. You tell yourself to wake up in two hours. Then you close your eyes and fall fast asleep.

Two hours later you wake up. Unicorn is playing with some of the kids at the park on the slide.

"Did you nap?" you ask. Then you yawn. It would have been nice to sleep for a couple more hours . . . or days. Maybe you can sleep for a week when this is all over.

Unicorn scuffs her hooves on the ground. "Maybe," she says.

Maybe. Or maybe not.

"You didn't sleep at all, did you?" you ask.

Unicorn actually looks relieved that you called her out. She bounces around and shoots a rainbow into the air from her horn. "Nope. Not at all!"

Winner of this round: DRAGON

Overall score: DRAGON 1 – UNICORN 2

Unicorn spins the wheel since you're still pretty tired from the nap. It goes around so fast you can't tell one thing from the next. Then it lands.

WALK THE DOG

Unicorn immediately backs up a few steps. "Um . . ."

You aren't sure what the big deal is. Walking a dog is easy.

"What's wrong?" you ask.

"I'm scared of dogs," Unicorn says.

Wow. That's too bad for Unicorn. But it's also kind of good for you. You will definitely win this round. You look around the park. There are at least five dogs of all sizes and colors. There's a really fun looking big dog over by the swing set. There's also a cute little dog by the bench.

If you walk the big dog, turn to page 128.

If you walk to small dog, turn to page 108.

"How about a swimming pool instead?" you say.

You and Dragon head to the local neighborhood swimming pool. There are a few kids splashing around.

Dragon shouts, "Cannonball!" and jumps.

The kids get out of the pool so quick, it's almost like they fly! Dragon lands in the water, making a huge splash. Water goes everywhere, covering you, the kids, and their parents. Then he flies out.

"Your turn, Unicorn," Dragon says.

You don't point out that he didn't really swim. And there are still a few inches of water left at the bottom of the pool. You jump in and start splashing around, having a great time. The kids rush over to you, and you carry them around on your back. Then you make the water turn an entire rainbow of colors. This is so much better than the ocean.

When you're done, you climb out of the pool.

"That wasn't technically swimming," Dragon says.

You fix your eyes on him and tap your hoof.

"Okay, fine, you win," Dragon says.

Winner of this round: UNICORN

Overall score: UNICORN 1 – DRAGON 2

"What's next?" Dragon says.

The crystal ball is dripping with water, but you wipe it off, and the two of you look inside.

Write A Poem

"Now we're talking," Dragon says. "I studied poetry for years."

You think he's kidding, but he doesn't sound like he's kidding. And sure, you can recite a silly little poem or two, but you never studied it. People who study poetry write serious poems that don't rhyme. People who haven't studied poetry write silly rhyming poems.

If you make up a serious poem, turn to page 130.

If you make up a silly poem, turn to page 124.

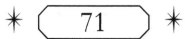

You totally did not mean to throw the beanbag there. It's not even on the numbers.

"Let me throw again," you say, and you stomp across the hopscotch board to get it.

Unicorn starts jumping up and down. "You can't walk on the chalk lines!" Unicorn says. "You lose!"

You look down at the chalk lines. Maybe that is one of the rules of hopscotch.

"I don't like hopscotch anyway," you say, and then you eat the beanbag.

Winner of this round: UNICORN

Overall score: DRAGON 2 – UNICORN 1

After you eat the beanbag, you burp. It smells like beans. This only makes you hungrier. Then you spin the wheel.

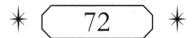

SET THE TABLE

"Set the table!" you say when the wheel stops spinning. "What table?"

Unicorn tosses her head up in the air, and the glitter goes flying. "I have a table back at my castle. We can go there and see who's better at setting the table."

This is already looking bad, but you aren't going to give up before you try.

You follow Unicorn back to her castle. It's shiny and sparkles just like Unicorn. You can barely fit through the door, but once you manage to squeeze yourself inside, you see the longest table you've ever seen in your life. There are stacks of plate and knives and forks, but you aren't sure what they're for.

"You set that side and I'll set this side," Unicorn says. Then she grabs a bunch of plates and starts putting them all over her side of the table.

If you copy what she's doing, turn to page 94.

If being sneaky is the better choice, turn to page 139.

You and Dragon agree to mess up a room for the other to clean up. You lead Dragon to two rooms that you love. One is your sunshine room and has yellow trinkets and pictures everywhere. The other is your rainbow room and has white poofy clouds and rainbow pencil holders and beanbag chairs.

You take the rainbow room and Dragon heads into the sunshine room. You try to cover your ears as you hear Dragon throwing stuff around. This was such a

bad idea. You don't like this contest.

That's okay. You can fix it.

As for you, you move a couple of the pencil holders around. You switch the yellow and green on every rainbow. You shift some of the clouds around. There. That should be good. He will never clean it up.

When you walk into the sunshine room, you can't believe what you see. The place is a complete wreck. It's a really good thing you are so good at cleaning. You get to work, and you put everything back in place. It takes you over an hour, but when you are done, it is perfect. Then you head back to the rainbow room to see how Dragon has done.

"You tried to trick me with the pencil holders, didn't you?" Dragon says.

"Maybe." But he did get them back in place. Still, that's about all he did.

"So I win?" Dragon asks.

"Nope. The rainbow colors are still wrong," you say. "Everyone knows that yellow comes before green."

"Does not," Dragon says.

You shoot out a rainbow and prove it to him.

Winner of this round: UNICORN

Overall score: UNICORN 2 – DRAGON 1

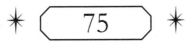

You look into the crystal ball, hoping the next contest is fun. This whole room-cleaning thing got you a little stressed out. The smoke swirls around, and when it clears, there is your next challenge.

Science Experiment

"Oh, I have a science lab we can use," you say.

You lead the way, stopping in the kitchen for a cookie break. Dragon eats an entire plate of cookies, but you love making cookies, so you'll just make some more later. Then you continue on to the lab.

Now, what kind of experiment to do? You could do something with rainbows and prisms because those are always great. Or you could do something on how to create glitter from biodegradable materials. It's hard to decide. You want to do whatever will help you win.

If you do the rainbow experiment, turn to page 122.

If you do the glitter experiment, turn to page 106.

You know so much about growing flowers. You definitely know that you can't grow flowers out of rocks. Or grow rock flowers. There is no such thing as rock flowers. Unless . . .

You hurry back to your castle and grab your giant bin of art supplies and take it to the park. You grab some rocks, and using your hot glue gun, you glue them together, making petals out of flat rocks and a nice circle rock for the center. Then you paint your creation pink and green, like a pretty flower. It looks so nice, and you make a few more. Then you sprinkle glitter over all of them.

They are perfect.

You bring them over to where Dragon sits on some rocks. He's blowing fire balls at the rocks. They're so hot that some of them glow bright red.

"The rock flowers won't grow!" Dragon says. You almost feel sorry for him. But you do want to win.

"Oh, I grew rock flowers," you say, and you present your creations.

Dragon narrows his eyes at them. "They aren't gold," he says.

"The rules never said they had to be," you say. Why is everything about gold for Dragon?

Winner of this round: UNICORN

Overall score: UNICORN 3 – DRAGON 0

This contest is almost in the bag. You look into the magic crystal ball and wait for the smoke to clear. It takes a while but finally settles.

Wash The Dishes

You jump up and down. "Oh, washing dishes means bubbles!" you say.

"Why do people wash dishes?" Dragon asks.

Is he serious?

"Because they're dirty," you say.

Dragon's eyes go wide and he smiles, exposing some very sharp fangs. You're really glad that dragons don't eat unicorns.

Wait! What if they do?

Well, if Dragon comes near you and tries to eat you, you can use your magic to turn him into a toad. But until then, it's time to wash dishes.

You and Dragon head to one of those all-you-can-eat buffets. People get a new plate every time they come through the line, and there are tons of people here. When you ask the dishwasher if you two can wash the dishes instead of him, he grins like he got a kitty cat. (Everyone loves kitties!)

Then you and Dragon get to work. You figure the best way to win is to not focus on what Dragon is doing and just do your very best work. But if you don't watch him, he might cheat.

If you watch Dragon, turn to page 90.

If you mind your own business, turn to page 154.

The last thing you want to paint are sunshine and flowers, but you do want to win. You pretend to be sparkly and happy like Unicorn, and you jab the brush into the brightest pink paint there is. You smear it across the canvas. It looks like a jellyfish. You add some blue, but then it looks like cotton candy. You try to blend it together with some green, and it looks like the lunch you just threw up. Unicorn is still busy painting, and she globs a bunch of yellow in the sky. You do the same. It reminds you of mustard and that makes you hungry. So you add some brown and white paint in your best version of a cow. This makes you even hungrier.

The more you paint, the hungrier you get. Finally you give up. You throw the paints and brush to the ground and eat the canvas. Then you pick the paints back up and eat those, too.

Unicorn looks over just as you burp.

"So I win?" Unicorn says. She's throwing a layer of glitter over her painting, making it sparkle just like her.

You burp again.

Winner of this round: <u>UNICORN</u>

Overall score: <u>DRAGON 1 – UNICORN 2</u>

You spin the wheel and watch it go around and around. Finally it lands.

FIND A TREASURE

No way! You are the best at finding a treasure. You can sniff out a treasure from miles away.

"I bet the treasure is at the end of the rainbow," Unicorn says.

You look up in the sky. "There is no rainbow."

"There will be," Unicorn says, then she runs and jumps across the soccer field at the park. Sure enough, she leaves behind a rainbow trail.

Okay, so that's a pretty neat trick, but it's not like there's going to magically be a treasure wherever she stops.

Except she is magic.

No, that's silly.

Unless it's not.

If you follow Unicorn and look for a treasure at the end of her rainbow trail, turn to page 88.

If you sniff out the treasure on your own, turn to page 126.

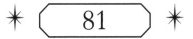

It takes a little convincing, but Unicorn finally agrees to go to the river in search of clay. She's sure you're trying to play a trick on her. You would never do that!

Okay, maybe you would, but this isn't a trick. And when you get to the river, you prove this to Unicorn. All along the bank of the river is a thick layer of clay. It's mushy, and your feet sink into it when you get there. You flop over on your back and look up at the sky.

Sometimes, when you want to get out of the cave for a little while, you come here and spend hours watching the sun cross the sky. The best part is that people always stay away from you, especially when you blow fire at them.

The last time you came here, you took the most amazing nap. You close your eyes and remember what it was like.

The next thing you know, someone is shaking your arm.

"Time is up," Unicorn says.

You open your eyes and look over to see a giant unicorn made out of clay. It's almost dry in the sun. And wait . . . the sun is way far across the sky from where it was. You must've fallen asleep . . . for hours.

Winner of this round: **UNICORN**

Overall score: **DRAGON 1 – UNICORN 2**

Somehow you've let Unicorn get ahead in the contest. But that's okay. You can still win no problem. You're a little bit tired, but you spin the wheel.

TAP DANCE

"What is that?" you ask Unicorn.

Unicorn laughs. "You don't know?"

Now you feel stupid. Maybe tap dancing is something everyone knows how to do.

"Of course I do," you say.

"Great," Unicorn says. "Go get your tap shoes and meet at the park." Then she bounds away, leaving a rainbow and glitter trail.

Well, this is an issue. You don't know what tap dancing is, and you definitely don't have shoes for it. You need to think of something.

If you fake it and pretend you know what you're doing, turn to page 96.

If you watch some how-to videos on the Internet, turn to page 98.

✳ 83 ✳

Y ou toss and turn, but you can't stop thinking about the alarm. Finally you get up and set an alarm. This way you will not oversleep and lose this contest. You can't afford to lose the contest.

You lie back down, but you can't figure out what position you were sleeping in that was so comfy. You shift around. You're still not comfortable. You pull a blanket over you. You take the blanket off. You try to count sheep, but all you want to do when you imagine them in your head is to eat them. It makes your stomach grumble. It grumbles so loudly that you can't fall asleep.

You're just about to change positions again when the alarm goes off. Unicorn jumps into your line of sight. "I slept for ten whole minutes!" she says. She's so full of energy and it's exhausting.

"Two more hours?" you say, because you really do want a nap.

"No time, Dragon," Unicorn says. "Get up!"

Winner of this round: UNICORN

Overall score: DRAGON 0 – UNICORN 3

This contest is not going the way you planned. You spin the wheel so hard it almost rolls away, but then it slows down and stops.

WATER THE PLANTS

What kind of contest is watering plants?

"Oh, I have an entire garden we can water," Unicorn says.

This you do not doubt. You follow Unicorn back to her castle. Sure enough around back is a garden.

Unicorn says, "How about you start on the left and I'll start on the right, and whoever gets to the middle first wins?"

This sounds okay to you.

"Oh, but make sure you don't step on the plants," Unicorn says. Then she bounds off to the right, grabs a watering can, and fills it from a hose.

If you're going to get to the middle first, you can't use a watering can. Your mouth is big enough to hold a huge amount of water. You can fill your mouth with water and water the plants that way. But maybe there's something Unicorn knows that you don't.

If you fill your mouth with water, turn to page 92.

If you use the watering can, turn to page 86.

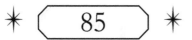

If you put the water in your mouth, you might destroy the plants. Not only will you lose the contest, it might also make Unicorn kind of sad because she really seems to like this garden.

You grab a watering can and fill it with water from the hose. Then you dump it on one plant. You do this again. And again. And it is taking forever. You're missing something important because Unicorn is almost done watering the plants and you aren't even past the first row.

You kind of glance at her out of the corner of your eye. Oh. She's using each can of water for at least ten plants. If you did that, you'd be going ten times faster (you are really good at math).

You start doing the same thing, but Unicorn is too far ahead. You go really fast, but it doesn't matter. You can't make up the time you've lost. And before you know it, Unicorn is at the center of the garden.

> **Winner of this round: UNICORN**
>
> **Overall score: DRAGON 0 – UNICORN 4**

Not only did you lose, it was a grand slam loss. You didn't win a single contest. This is the worst humiliation you have ever faced in your life.

You almost blow flames all over the garden, but then Unicorn prances over to you.

"Hey Dragon, do you want to go get ice cream?" she says.

Ice cream sound amazing. So you agree. You can set the garden on fire after the ice cream . . . maybe. Or maybe you can try the whole contest again.

THE END

Maybe there is treasure at the end of the rainbow. And unicorns are magical. Unicorn might be able to make treasure and find it. You can't let that happen. You have to get to it first.

You run after Unicorn, sticking so close that glitter gets all over you. The world becomes a giant rainbow blur, but you keep her in your sight. Unicorn bounces up and down all over the park. Then she moves in a giant circle, forming a rainbow/glitter cloud. It gets up your nose and you sneeze.

When you stop sneezing, you can't find Unicorn anywhere. The rainbow/glitter cloud is too thick to see through, and you try to run out of it. But you don't know which way you came from. You can't even see the kids and the swing sets anymore at the park.

You stumble through the rainbow dust and finally see light coming from the other side. The rainbow dust clears and you find yourself back on the soccer field.

There is Unicorn sitting next to a giant pot of gold.

"Did you find a treasure also?" Unicorn asks. She's trying to sound all innocent, but it's obvious that's she's pushing your buttons. You think about stealing her treasure and flying away because the gold is super shiny, but it also smells like a leprechaun (which smells like dirty feet).

You grumble something in response, but no matter what you say, the contest is over.

Winner of this round: UNICORN

Overall score: DRAGON 1 – UNICORN 3

Unicorn is the winner! This is humiliating! How could you have let a unicorn win? The only thing to do is to have a rematch. Then you'll really show that you are better.

THE END

You definitely need to keep an eye on Dragon. You turn away for a minute, just to get set up. You fill your sink with water and soap, making sure there are plenty of bubbles. Then you pick up the first dish and start washing it. While it's soaking in the bubbly water, you turn back to look at Dragon.

He is almost done washing the dishes! How is that even possible? You haven't heard him turn on the water, and there isn't a bubble in sight. But his stack of clean dishes is huge. He picks up the final dish he has left to wash . . . and he licks it clean!

Ugh! That is just gross!

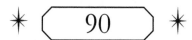

"You can't lick the dishes!" you shout. How could he think that was okay?

"Why not?" Dragon says, and he finishes licking it and sets it down with the rest of the clean dishes.

"Because . . . because . . ." Why hadn't you set rules?

Dragon picks up one of the clean dishes, and you have to admit that it sparkles. This is not fair. But he's also done and you aren't.

> **Winner of this round: DRAGON**
>
> **Overall score: UNICORN 3 – DRAGON 1**

Okay. Fine. Maybe he won this round. But you won the overall contest. You are the best. You vow never to eat from dishes that Dragon serves you. But how will you know? Maybe other dragons lick dishes clean. Or people. It's too much to think about. You are going to have to wash every dish you ever eat with from now on. That's all there is to it.

The End

You hurry over to the hose, but instead of filling the watering can, you put the hose in your mouth and turn it on full blast. You swallow a bunch of water, but you still keep the water on until your mouth will burst if you put any more water in it. Then you turn to the plants.

You stand on the side and you spray water all over them. The water goes everywhere, like a huge rainstorm, but when you're done, you've watered over half the plants you need to water.

You fill your mouth again and water the rest of the plants. Then you fly over to the middle of the garden so you won't step on any plants, and you land.

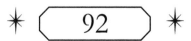

Unicorn isn't even halfway done. You wait and you watch. She sings songs and talks to the plants, and even though she's not going to win this contest, she still seems to be having a great time. You think there might be a lesson here, but whatever. It doesn't matter. You win.

Winner of this round: <u>DRAGON</u>

Overall score: <u>DRAGON 1 – UNICORN 3</u>

Sure, you win this round, but you lose the entire contest. Unicorn wins. That stinks.

"I demand another contest," you tell Unicorn. Then you turn back to the beginning of the book and start all over.

THE END

You grab a stack of plates and slam them down on the table, one after another, just like Unicorn is doing. A bunch of them break, but you can't do anything about that now. You set napkins down, but you accidentally sneeze and flames come out your nose and set some of them on fire. You grab knives and forks and spoons, and you try to put them down just like Unicorn, but they're shiny and gold, and you keep tucking them inside your pockets.

When you look up, Unicorn is watching you.

"I think I won this round," she says.

At least you got the shiny silverware.

> **Winner of this round: UNICORN**
>
> **Overall score: DRAGON 2 – UNICORN 2**

Oh, no! It's a tie!

Turn to page 132 for the tie-breaker.

I f you suggest another game, Dragon is going to think you're scared. And you might be scared of scary stuff, like puppies and thunder, but you are not scared of some silly little video game. After all, how hard can it be?

Dragon goes first. It's some flying game where you have to look for all the enemies and zap them with fire. Dragon never misses a single target. His turn lasts for ten minutes, and he only loses when you "accidentally" step on his toes with your hoof. (No, really. It was an accident. You would never do that on purpose!)

"Doesn't matter," Dragon says, and then it's your turn.

You lose within the first thirty seconds.

"This game is no fun at all!" you say. You know you sound like you're pouting, but it's really not fun.

"It's fun if you're good at it," Dragon says.

Winner of this round: DRAGON

Overall score: UNICORN 2 – DRAGON 2

It's a tie! You may have lost at this video game thing, but you still have a chance to show Dragon how amazing you are!

Turn to page 134 for the tie-breaker.

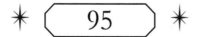

Y ou don't know what tap dancing is, but you certainly don't have time to figure it out. Instead you sit down on a bench at the park and wait for Unicorn to get back.

"You broke the bench," Unicorn says when she returns.

Underneath you is a pile of wood. Oops.

"Why don't you go first?" you say to Unicorn. You can watch her and then maybe you can do whatever she does.

Unicorn can hardly wait. She straps some little pieces of metal to her hooves and she prances up to the pavilion stage at the park. Then she starts moving all four of her legs, making a musical racket each time the metal touches the floor.

Fine, it's not a complete racket. It's actually kind of awesome. It's also impossible. There is no way you can do that. You don't even have tap shoes like Unicorn.

"Did you like it?" Unicorn asks when she's done.

You grumble something about how she wasn't bad. She sparkles with happiness.

Now it's your turn.

"Can I borrow your shoes?" you ask Unicorn.

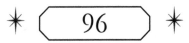

You don't expect her to say yes, but she unstraps them and you put them on. The first step you take you fall on your face. This is worse than that time you tried roller skating. How can anyone dance in these things?

Winner of this round: UNICORN

Overall score: DRAGON 1 – UNICORN 3

Unicorn wins! Then Unicorn says, "Do you want me to teach you how to tap dance?"

You think she's messing with you, but her eyes are huge and hopeful and learning how to do the cool dance moves would make you even more awesome than you are.

"I guess," you say.

And you spend the rest of the afternoon there in the park.

THE END

If you want to have any chance of winning this competition, you need to try your hardest. You climb out of the clay and shake off, throwing clay everywhere. It gets all over some woman, and she seems kind of upset. She seems even more upset when you ask if you can use her phone to watch tap dancing videos. You blow a little smoke her way, just to scare her, and finally she agrees.

You sit down next to the woman at the park and she plays a video called *"Anyone can Tap Dance."* Some guy in funny shoes that make a lot of noise dances around. He also sings. You watch the video. Then you watch another. And another. It looks like so much fun. You can't wait to try it yourself.

Luckily you don't have to wait long. Unicorn runs back up, but every step she makes, it has the clicking sound like in the video.

"Are you ready, Dragon?" she asks.

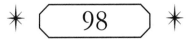

You are as ready as you will ever be.

Unicorn goes first, and she isn't half bad. She isn't half good either. Her feet make the right sounds, but she kind of looks like she's walking over hot coals. Her legs go every direction possible. She won't be putting any *"How-to"* videos on the Internet for people to watch.

When she's done, you stand up and look around the park, trying to spot something you can use as tap shoes. Oh, the pavilion nearby has a metal roof. You rip off a couple of metal shingles and strap them to your feet. Then you dance just like the guy in the video.

Pretty soon, kids stop playing and watch you. Some mom starts videotaping you. Maybe she'll put a video on the Internet. You can be famous.

You're having so much fun that it takes you three songs before you notice Unicorn trying to stop you. You finally stop dancing.

"Show off," Unicorn says.

Winner of this round: DRAGON

Overall score: DRAGON 2 – UNICORN 2

Sweet! You tied it! Now to win.

Turn to page 132 for the tie-breaker.

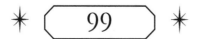

Y ou need to go first. Otherwise Unicorn might use up all the music in the piano.

"I got this," you say, and you sit on the bench. It breaks into pieces. Oops. Then you tap your claws in the white and black keys. Oh! Each time you touch one, there is a sound. You tap them over and over, harder each time because it's really cool and makes you sound like someone named Beethoven. (You should have used that in your DRAGON name! BEETHOVEN THE CREATOR OF MUSIC AND THE DESTROYER OF SILENCE. Now that is a cool name!)

When you think you've used as much of the music as you can, you step back.

"I've never heard that song before," Unicorn says.

You think fast. "I made it up myself," you say.

"You compose music, too?" she says.

You don't know what composing is, but you smile and nod.

Then Unicorn hits her hooves on the white and black keys and taps something that sounds like chopsticks being thrown on the ground. It makes you hungry.

When she's done, she slams her hooves down one last time. All the white and black keys fly everywhere. Unicorn cringes and looks around to see if anyone is watching.

"I think you won," Unicorn says.

You think so, too.

Winner of this round: DRAGON

Overall score: DRAGON 3 – UNICORN 1

You won! You are the best. You try not to do a victory dance, but you can't help yourself. Dragons Rule!

THE END

You realize that you like cleaning toilets in your castle, not at gross, smelly places.

"How about we don't clean?" you say. This way it will be a tie and you can figure out a different contest to have.

"Works for me," Dragon says. Then he blows fire out of his mouth right at the bathrooms. They explode into a ball of flames.

"What did you do?" you ask, stepping back so the flames don't get into your fancy rainbow hair.

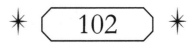

Dragon brushes ash off his scales. "I got rid of the entire mess. Which means I won."

"But I thought we agreed not to clean?" you say. This is not how you imagined the contest ending.

"Did we?" Dragon says. "Well, I guess I changed my mind."

Winner of this round: DRAGON

Overall score: UNICORN 1 – DRAGON 3

Oh no! Dragon won! And nobody can even use the toilets. But actually, maybe they were better off being burned. They were the worst you'd ever seen.

"I'm heading back to the other park," you say. "You know, the one with the clean toilets." This is about as much competition as you can handle for one day.

Or is it?

The End

You are so good at counting gold, but if you just focus on that, you are for sure going to get the answer wrong. How much gold is there in a destroyed town? Well, if the town has one hundred people and they each have one piece of gold, then that's one hundred more pieces of gold. But sometimes people have more than one piece of gold. Maybe every other person has two pieces of gold. Oh, it's so confusing, but it's got to be factored in. So you add an extra one hundred fifty pieces of gold to the answer.

"Two hundred ninety-four," you say.

Unicorn looks up from where she's scratching marks in the ground. You were able to do everything in your head. You are that good at math.

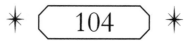

"That's not what I got," Unicorn says. "It's one hundred forty-four."

She obviously didn't take the destroyed town into account. She is so wrong.

You flip the question over. On the back is the answer: one hundred forty-four.

Winner of this round: UNICORN

Overall score: DRAGON 2 – UNICORN 2

A tie!

You can't believe that you're actually tied. This is the worst. As if Unicorn doesn't already thing she's the best at everything, now she's about to win. You can't let that happen.

Turn to page 132 for the tie-breaker.

Rainbows are great, but you've already shown off your rainbow skills. For this science experiment, you are going to make biodegradable glitter.

You run out to your garden and grab some eucalyptus leaves. They make the best glitter, and when you throw the glitter everywhere, it won't hurt the environment.

You hurry back to the science lab, because you don't want to leave Dragon alone for too long. He's sitting in front of a burning ball of fire that's floating in the air.

"What do you think, Unicorn?" Dragon says.

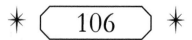

It's actually a pretty cool trick. It would win . . . maybe . . . if you didn't have this glitter thing.

"Nice. But watch this," you say. Then you put the leaves on the table and go to the supply cabinet for more materials. When you get back, the leaves are gone.

Dragon burps. It smells like eucalyptus.

"You ate the leaves!" you say. You can't believe Dragon.

"They were tasty," he says. "And I guess that means I win."

It means nothing of the sort, but you don't want to lose your temper. Maybe he was just really hungry (even though he ate an entire plate of cookies).

Winner of this round: <u>DRAGON</u>

Overall score: <u>UNICORN 2 – DRAGON 2</u>

Oh no! It's a tie! You have one last chance to show Dragon you are the best!

Turn to page 134 for the tie-breaker.

Walking the big dog is a risk. He might try to run away, and then you'd look really mean yanking on his leash. Walking the small dog is a much better idea.

You head over toward the tiny little dog. It barks at you. You move closer and it barks some more. Pretty soon it won't stop barking. You want to cover your ears because it's so loud and high-pitched. Then every other dog in the park starts barking, too, and pretty soon the place is chaos. What is it with little dogs and barking?

Oh, wait. Now that you think about it, you remember this happening once before. Maybe twice before. Little dogs bark a lot.

So much for walking a dog. But Unicorn can't be doing much better. You head back to where you left her. She's prancing around with a stuffed animal on her back.

"Look, Dragon!" she says. "I'm walking the dog."

The stuffed animal is a dog!

"That's not—" you start.

She prances over to you. "The rules didn't say that the dog had to be a 'real' dog."

Stupid rules.

Winner of this round: UNICORN

Overall score: DRAGON 1 – UNICORN 3

Unicorn wins! You grumble something about eating the stuffed animal, but then some little kid runs up and Unicorn hands it back to him. The kid runs off, leaving you and Unicorn to decide what to do next.

"Rematch?" you say.

"Definitely."

THE END

UNICORN

S ure, you are a magical creature, but using magic to win just doesn't seem right. You miss every single hoop. After Dragon has made fifty and you've made zero, you finally give up. It's time to move on to the next contest.

Winner of this round: DRAGON

Overall score: UNICORN 2 – DRAGON 2

It's a tie! You have one final chance to show Dragon that you are amazing and awesome and the best at everything . . . except the things you've lost at so far. But everything else.

Turn to page 134 for the tie-breaker.

You jump super high. As high as you can possibly jump. But you ate a lot for dinner last night and you hardly make it three inches off the ground.

"Pretty sure I jumped higher," Unicorn says.

You grumble and growl and blow smoke from your nostrils because it's really hard to admit defeat. But there is no getting around it.

"Fine," you say. "You flew better."

Inwardly you grumble. Neither of you flew. But whatever. The results are in.

Winner of this round: <u>UNICORN</u>

Overall score: <u>DRAGON 3 – UNICORN 1</u>

You are the winner! You may have lost this round, but overall you are the best (of course).

THE END

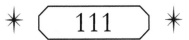

"How about this game instead?" you suggest, and you point to the one with the sparkles where you do dance moves.

Dragon grumbles. "No way. That's your favorite game I bet."

Fine. You won't play your favorite game and you won't play his. You ask some kid to recommend a game, and she suggests some old-school game with little shapes you have to fit together. The best part is you get to play at the same time and you get the same pieces.

Dragon is really good at the game. So are you. You stack pieces perfectly just like you would if you were building a colorful brick wall. But Dragon is stacking his pieces perfectly also. This could go on forever. If you want to win, you are going to have to be creative.

The hardest piece shows up on the screen. You say, "Is that a pile of gold over there by the mini-golf course?"

"Where?" Dragon says, and he looks away.

That's all it takes. You place the piece. He doesn't. Then it's all over for Dragon. He tries to recover, but that one little piece ruined everything.

Winner of this round: UNICORN

Overall score: UNICORN 3 – DRAGON 1

You win! You knew you were better than Dragon. But Dragon pulls two more quarters from his pocket and demands a rematch. Who are you to say no? After all there are way worse things you could be doing besides playing video games with your new best friend, Dragon.

The End

You grab your perfect milkshake recipe and you get to work. The ice cream shop has so many flavors, but you know that sticking with one is going to win you this contest. You decide on Buttercup Sunshine. It's always been one of your favorites. You add the perfect amount of milk. Then you decide on one more flavor to add. Nothing that will hide the delicious taste of the sunshine. You pick out Creamy Cupcake flavoring and you add just a pinch. With a spoon, you take a small taste.

It is perfect!

"Try this!" you say, turning around to face Dragon.

He's normally red, but right now he's green and lying on the ground looking like he's going to be sick.

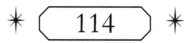

"I ate the ice cream," Dragon manages to say.

"Is that bad?" you ask.

"I'm lactose intolerant," he says.

Again, you aren't sure what it means, but maybe it's why he turned green. You do know one thing it means.

You won!

Winner of this round: <u>UNICORN</u>

Overall score: <u>UNICORN 2 – DRAGON 2</u>

A tie! This is not good. You should have won the entire contest by now. You drink the milkshake and then get ready for the tie-breaker.

Turn to page 134 for the tie-breaker.

Letting Unicorn go first is a good strategy. Then you'll know exactly how good you need to be. Also it can't be hard to play a piano better than a unicorn.

"Go ahead," you say, and you plop down on the ground to listen to the music.

Unicorn smashes her hooves down on the piano keys and a loud mishmash of music fills the air. The black and white keys fly everywhere. You count them as they fly through the air. There are eighty-eight of them.

Unicorn jumps up and shoots rainbows everywhere, making it look like a piano rainbow explosion.

"Your turn!" she says.

Your mouth falls open. She can't be serious.

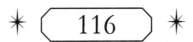

"You destroyed the piano," you say. "I can't play that."

"So I win?!" Unicorn says.

This is ridiculous. You almost suggest finding a different piano so you can win, but then you remember that you can't play piano anyway. You can win the next round.

Winner of this round: UNICORN

Overall score: DRAGON 2 – UNICORN 2

Wait! It's a tie! You should have tried to find another piano. You better win the next round.

Turn to page 132 for the tie-breaker.

You normally use only one flavor in your milkshakes, but if you are going to win, you need to be better than normal. You decide to use three different flavors. But what three flavors?

The best thing to do is to try each flavor. You start on the left and have a spoon of each one. There is banana and strawberry and chocolate chip cookie dough. You're getting a little full, but if you don't try them all, you might not pick out the perfect three flavors.

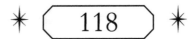

You try four more flavors. Five more. Ten more. You try for one more, but the thought of any more ice cream makes you want to throw up. And the thought of making a milkshake is even worse. There is no way you can bring yourself to do it.

You turn to Dragon. He has a lump of vanilla ice cream sitting in a cup of milk.

"Do I win?" he asks.

You nod. You feel too sick to actually speak.

Winner of this round: DRAGON

Overall score: UNICORN 1 – DRAGON 3

Dragon wins! This is the worst! You've been defeated by a dragon. You want to try again, but first you need to feel a little bit better.

The End

"It's not that bad," you say to Dragon even though it really is that bad. "We have to clean."

You put on gloves, power up your unicorn rainbow magic, and get to work. You also don't breathe until you are done. But when you finally walk out of your side of the toilets, they are sparkling, just like you. This was definitely a situation where magic was required. And you have to win this contest if you want any chance of winning the competition.

Dragon hasn't moved.

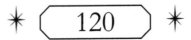

"So I win," you say, brushing glitter off the cleaning gloves.

"You win," Dragon says.

You dance around with happiness.

Dragon doesn't seem the least bit upset. He says, "Unicorn, I may be great at pretty much everything, but I am happy that you are better at cleaning toilets."

You aren't sure how you feel about that.

Winner of this round: UNICORN

Overall score: UNICORN 2 – DRAGON 2

Whew! You brought it back to a tie! One last chance to show Dragon that you are the best.

Turn to page 134 for the tie-breaker.

Glitter is fun, but to win, you need to go with the rainbows. After all, rainbows are your specialty.

You get to work, filling a bowl with water and finding a nice glass prism. Then you help the water get a little misty, and you get a light. The more rainbows the better. You shine the light in both the mist and through the prism.

Rainbows explode around the science lab! Then you turn on your disco ball, and they go everywhere, dancing around like they are alive.

"What do you think of that, Dragon?" you say. "Aren't they epic!?"

"Epic," Dragon says. "But watch this."

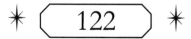

He proceeds to lie down and fall asleep.

You try to wake him up, but he sleeps for an entire day. When he finally wakes, he says, "Did I win?"

"Doing what?" you ask.

"Hibernating," Dragon says.

You explain that he was supposed to do a science experiment, not *be* a science experiment, and thus you win.

Winner of this round: UNICORN

Overall score: UNICORN 3 – DRAGON 1

Funny enough, Dragon is not all that bothered. He eats another plate of cookies and then proceeds to fall back asleep. You think about suggesting he go back to his own cave if he's going to hibernate, but you decide that first you'll make some more cookies.

The End

Maybe serious poets write serious poems, but you are not a serious poet. It you do that, it will be awful. Maybe your silly poem will be awful, too, but at least it will be happy.

You go first.

"Unicorn and Dragon were playing at the park.
Dragon was scared because it was getting dark."

"I'm not scared of the dark," Dragon says.

"Shhh . . . ," you say. Then you keep going.

"Dragon lit a fire and brightened up the night.
Then Unicorn made cupcakes and they ate them by
the light."

You take a bow when you are done. That was a great poem if you do say so yourself.

"It's a fake poem," Dragon says. "I would never be scared of the dark."

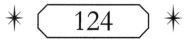

You shrug because it doesn't really matter as far as you can tell.

"Are you going to go?" you ask Dragon.

"Fine," Dragon says. "But two can play at that game." Then he begins.

> *"Unicorns are scared of mice.*
> *Unicorns are scared of lice.*
> *Unicorns are scared of dice.*
> *Unicorns are scared of rice.*
> *Unicorns are scared of ice."*

He blows out a ball of fire at the end then bows.

"Umm . . . is that what they taught you in poetry school?" you ask.

"Nope."

So you win.

Winner of this round: <u>UNICORN</u>

Overall score: <u>UNICORN 2 – DRAGON 2</u>

Oh no! A tie. Dragon is already grumpy. Now you'll have to do one more contest to see who is the best.

Turn to page 134 for the tie-breaker.

You aren't following some made-up rainbow searching for a treasure. You are a mighty dragon! You have found so much treasure in your life, you can hardly count it all. You lift your nose into the fresh outdoor air and sniff. It only takes you a second. Gold. Pure gold. You would recognize the smell anywhere. And it's not far off. If fact it you aren't mistaken (and you rarely are), it is right here at the park.

You creep along quietly because if someone is protecting the gold, you don't want them to hear you coming. Ahead are three parents sitting on a bench together. The gold must be buried under the bench. You jump up high and land right in front of them, roaring as loudly as you can.

They shriek and start to run away. But when the one in the middle opens her mouth, you see a gold tooth inside.

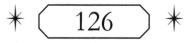

That's the treasure! The gold tooth.

You almost reach into her mouth and pull it out, but then you remember something about that not being very nice. So instead you ask her if you can pull her gold tooth out and have it.

"No way," she says.

Who's not being nice now?

You have two options: pull the tooth out or take her with you back to Unicorn. It's a hard decision, but you finally ask her (very nicely) if she'll come with you to see Unicorn.

She agrees. Maybe she's just scared you'll eat her.

Unicorn is still looking for gold when you find her and show her the gold tooth.

"That's not a treasure," Unicorn says.

Gold is gold, and this tooth is definitely a treasure.

Winner of this round: DRAGON

Overall score: DRAGON 2 – UNICORN 2

But wait! It's a tie!

There has to be a way for you to defeat Unicorn.

Turn to page 132 for the tie-breaker.

You decide to walk the big dog. The little dog looks so small, you worry you might get it stuck between your toes. The big dog spots you and barks one time, then it starts wagging its tail.

The owner is really nice and she hands you the leash, and you set out across the soccer field walking the dog. There are some kids playing soccer, but they make sure not to kick the ball at you or the dog.

The dog keeps wagging its tail, and it acts like it's having the best time in the world. You wonder how Unicorn is doing. When you get back, you find out. Unicorn hasn't moved near any of the dogs. She's backed away from all of them and fear fills her eyes.

"What do you think will happen if you walk one of the dogs?" you ask.

"I don't want to find out!" Unicorn says.

Winner of this round: <u>DRAGON</u>

Overall score: <u>DRAGON 2 – UNICORN 2</u>

It's a tie! You can seriously win this contest. I mean, you thought you were going to win easily, but somehow Unicorn has done okay. That's fine though. You still have one more chance.

Turn to page 132 for the tie-breaker.

If Dragon is that good at poetry, then you need to at least try to be serious. Dragon goes first, and you can't lie. His poem is really great. It's about gold and treasures and scary things, but it also creates such vivid images in your mind. It's almost like that is what poetry is supposed to do. And it makes you *feel* so sad. You never knew you could feel that way about a poem.

"Your turn," Dragon says.

Here goes nothing. You stand up and start making up a non-rhyming, serious poem on the spot.

"Rainbow.
Thunder on a mountain.
I yearn to bring them together.
I never will."

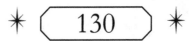

Whew. That took everything out of you.

Dragon raises an eyebrow at you. "Do you think your poem was better than mine, Unicorn?"

Oh, you want to say yes. You want to win. But you just can't do it.

"No." Dragon's poem was way better.

Winner of this round: DRAGON

Overall score: UNICORN 1 – DRAGON 3

Wait! You should have tried harder. Now Dragon has won the entire competition. And you know you are better than him, at least at some things. The only fair thing to do would be to try the entire contest again.

The End

You and Unicorn are tied. This competition has been way harder than you ever thought it would be.

Unicorn spins the wheel. It goes around and around and finally stops.

BUILD A SANDCASTLE

"Oh, I live in a castle," Unicorn says. "This will be easy."

Unicorn may live in a castle, but you've attacked plenty of castles in your day. This should be easy for you, too.

You and Unicorn head to the beach. The sun is shining, and it makes your scales feel nice and warm. It would be super amazing to lie down and take a nap in the sunshine.

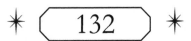

"Ten minutes and we see who makes the best one," Unicorn says. Then she starts digging up sand with her hooves and tossing it everywhere. A bunch of it hits you in the face. You almost get mad, but then you remember that you only have ten minutes to build an amazing sandcastle.

You move away and start digging through the sand. It's warm and you roll around in it. It sure would be great to close your eyes and relax.

If you close your eyes, just for a second, turn to page 138.

If you build as fast as you can, turn to page 142.

If you take your time and try to make your castle perfect, turn to page 152.

I t is a tie. If you don't win this last contest, then Dragon will never stop talking about how amazing he is. You can't believe you let him win anything, not to mention tie this whole thing with you. Unicorns are magical and sparkly. Dragons aren't. Wait, maybe magic and sparkles aren't the answer to everything.

No, that's silly. Of course they are.

You and Dragon look into the crystal ball for the next and final challenge.

Dress in Costume

"Yes!" you say. Costumes and unicorns were meant to be together. You almost dash off to your costume closet, but wait. You need to think this through. You have to win.

If you dress is the most sparkly costume you have, turn to page 156.

If you dress in a mashup costume, turn to page 148.

If you dress in a totally new costume, turn to page 144.

Hip Hop is the way to go. You flip down your sunglasses and slide onto the dance floor. You spin around like you're break dancing. You do the splits. You balance on your front legs. You move to the beat perfectly. The people clap for each beat of the song and you cater to them, waving and spinning and being your completely awesome unicorn self.

You end in a headstand and shoot out some rainbows.

The crowd erupts in cheers.

Dragon hangs his head. You are definitely better at dancing.

Winner of this round: UNICORN

Overall score: UNICORN 1 – DRAGON 3

Wait. Maybe you are better at dancing, but Dragon won the entire competition. Oh, the shame. To let a dragon beat you. You are going to tell Dragon that you want a rematch, but first, why not dance for the crowd one more time?

The End

Jumping is not going to win you this contest. But without your wings you aren't going to be able to fly either. Unless you try something different.

You look down at the ground and blow out a huge stream of fire. So much fire that it pushes you up into the air, way higher than Unicorn went.

"Look at that!" you shout down at Unicorn. "I'm flying without my wings."

"How are you going to land?" Unicorn shouts back up at you.

Land? You hadn't thought that far into the future.

You stop blowing out the fire and you fall, down, down, down until you land hard. Everything around you shakes. A couple of buildings fall over, but they were kind of ugly anyway so no one will miss them.

"Guess I won," you say, jumping out of the crater formed by your impact.

"But that landing," Unicorn says.

You point out that landing was not part of the contest.

Winner of this round: DRAGON

Overall score: DRAGON 4 – UNICORN 0

You win! You are the best! You knew it. And now Unicorn knows it, too!

THE END

You close your eyes, just for a second. The sun just feels so good. You have ten whole minutes. Closing your eyes for one of them won't hurt. But the next thing you know, Unicorn is waking you up.

You look over to see a sandcastle bigger than you are. You can't believe Unicorn built that in ten minutes.

"Did you build a sandcastle in your sleep?" Unicorn says. She sounds like she's making fun of you which is really annoying.

You try to think of something witty and funny to say, but you got nothing. So you only shake your head and say, "Nice castle."

> **Winner of this round: <u>UNICORN</u>**
>
> **Overall score: <u>DRAGON 2 – UNICORN 3</u>**

Unicorn is the winner! Oh, it is so not fair! You demand a rematch.

The End

You have no idea how to set a table, and even if you copied Unicorn, it probably wouldn't end well. She sets a final fork down and then says, "I'm done. And I guess I win."

You shake your head, wishing you had glitter fly everywhere when you did it because that would be pretty cool. Then you say, "Watch this."

Unicorn watches as you grab the entire table and turn it on its side. Dishes slide off, smashing on the ground. Then you set the table down on its side.

"There," you say. "I set the table . . . on its side."

Unicorn's mouth falls open. "But I set the table."

You point to the smashed dishes. "Doesn't look like it. And I guess that means I won."

> **Winner of this round: DRAGON**
>
> **Overall score: DRAGON 3 – UNICORN 1**

You won! Sure, maybe that was a cheap trick, but that's ancient history. And Unicorn can always ask for a rematch, anyway.

THE END

Magical

If you want any chance of winning at a hoop shooting contest, you are going to need to use magic. And you are a unicorn after all. Unicorns have magic! It's not cheating if it is part of who you are.

Dragon shoots . . . and makes it.

You shoot and use magic . . . and make it. Yes! This is perfect. Except he's already ahead by one, and you need to win.

The next time he shoots the ball, you use your magic again, just to make the wind blow . . . really strong.

The ball veers off course and misses. The second time you do this, Dragon looks at you suspiciously.

"Are you doing that, Unicorn?" he asks.

You look as innocent as you can and shake your head. "It's just kind of windy today."

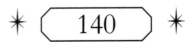

So it's a tiny white lie. But this contest matters. And you can't lose. You can make cookies for Dragon as a way to say you're sorry once you win. And now you are ahead. At the end of the hoop shooting contest, you are declared the winner.

Winner of this round: <u>UNICORN</u>

Overall score: <u>UNICORN 3 – DRAGON 1</u>

You knew you were better than Dragon, and this contest only proves it. Dragon doesn't even seem all that mad. He asks if you want to shoot hoops a little more, just for fun, and you agree. You miss every single one.

The End

You build the castle as fast as you can. You dig through the sand with your claws and throw all the extra sand behind you. You mush it all together into a big blob. Better to make it as big as possible and then you can fine-tune it later on. After all, you have ten whole minutes.

Well only six minutes left now.

You keep digging.

Finally a timer goes off. The ten minutes is up.

You look over your sand castle. It looks like a giant blob of sand. Uh oh. Maybe you should have hurried up and added some more details.

Slowly you turn around, ready to face your defeat. But all Unicorn has is a giant blob also. Oh wait, she also has a really sour look on her face, like she ate a lemon.

"You threw sand all over my castle," Unicorn says.

You shrug, throwing more sand everywhere. "It looks pretty good to me."

Unicorn kicks at it. "But it was better."

As far as you're concerned, if her castle was better, that's in the past.

> **Winner of this round: <u>NEITHER</u>**
>
> **Overall score: <u>DRAGON 2 – UNICORN 2</u>**

You almost suggest another tie-breaker because you're feeling pretty confident, but then Unicorn bounds away, leaving rainbows as a trail. She's kind of being a sore loser. Oh well. You have bigger problems to worry about . . . but you decide to take a nice nap there in the sand first.

THE END

Costumes are the best when they are fresh and new. You rush off to your costume-making room and you begin. You use all your craft supplies to pull together the best costume you can think of. It has so many parts, and you make sure each one is perfect. Then you put it on and hurry back to the park.

Dragon's mouth drops open when he sees you. "You're a . . ."

"I'm a dragon," you say. But you aren't just any dragon. You are Dragon.

"I love it so much!" Dragon says. "It's the best costume in the world!"

Dragon is dressed as Little Bo Peep and looks pretty darling, but who are you to disagree with him?

Winner of this round: UNICORN

Overall score: UNICORN 3 – DRAGON 2

You win! And Dragon is so happy and flattered that you dressed as him that he treats you to a funnel cake from one of the nearby food trucks. People take all sorts of pictures of the two of you, and pretty soon you've gone viral on social media. You celebrate by having another funnel cake.

The End

You do the math quickly in your head, just like you're counting gold back at your cave. The destroyed town . . . it is definitely there to trick you.

"One hundred forty-four," you say.

Unicorn is still scribbling out hoof marks on the ground. "Are you sure?"

"Of course I'm sure. That's my answer. What's yours?"

Unicorn scratches out all the marks. "One thousand days of sunshine."

There is a tiny tiny chance you are wrong, but her answer definitely isn't right either.

You flip over the question, and on the back is one hundred forty-four, just like you said.

"I knew it!" you say, even though you didn't.

> **Winner of this round: DRAGON**
>
> **Overall score: DRAGON 3 – UNICORN 1**

You won!

"Told you I'd win," you say.

"This time, maybe," Unicorn says. "But there is always next time."

THE END

Mashup costumes are the best. You have so many costumes in your costume closet, but of them, you pick some of your favorites. You decide on your princess, superhero, astronaut, and video game character costumes and you mash them all together into one costume. It is perfect.

Or is it too much? Maybe you should make it only a princess superhero mashup. Or a superhero astronaut mashup? Oh, it's so hard to tell. No, all four is the best.

You hurry back to the park.

Dragon is dressed as a princess! It's amazing! It's awesome! It's—

Oh, wait. You want to win this contest.

"What are you?" Dragon asks.

"I'm a princess, superhero, astronaut, video game character," you say proudly.

He looks very skeptical.

"Too much?" you ask.

"Too much," Dragon says.

You should have just gone with two of the four.

Winner of this round: <u>DRAGON</u>

Overall score: <u>UNICORN 2 – DRAGON 3</u>

Dragon wins the entire competition! It's unfair. But then he dances around in his princess costume and you can't help but be happy.

THE END

Ballet is definitely the answer. You grab your toe shoes and you tie them onto all four feet. Then you put on your favorite tutu. You also cover the dance floor with glitter so the place will really sparkle. Then you start dancing.

You twirl around. You jump and spin. You kick your legs out. You balance on your toes. And then . . . you slip on glitter and fall flat on the ground. All four of your legs splay out to the side.

"Are you okay?" one of the people asks.

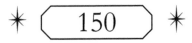

You don't think you broke anything. But you do think you lost the dance contest.

> **Winner of this round: <u>DRAGON</u>**
>
> **Overall score: <u>UNICORN 0 – DRAGON 4</u>**

This is the worst. Not only did you lose the competition, you lost every single challenge. And you know that you're so good at so many things.

"Dragon?" you say. "Do you want to go watch a movie?" You are very good at watching movies.

"I'm better at watching movies than you," Dragon says.

Doubt. But after your humiliating defeat, it will be nice to hide in a dark theater for a while. Then, maybe after that, you can try the contest again.

THE END

If you are going to win this sandcastle contest, you need to make your castle perfect. You start at the lowest level of the castle, maybe the most important level: the dungeon. All castles need a strong dungeon. If not, then how are they going to lock up prisoners? And sure, this is just a sandcastle, but that doesn't mean it's not important. You carve every stone with your sharp claws. But then you realize that the dungeon isn't big enough, so you make it wider. And you add another level.

Behind you an alarm goes off.

Unicorn bounds over. "Is that all you got done?"

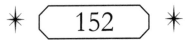

You turn to see a massive sandcastle behind her.

It's okay. You got this.

"Yes," you say. "But look at the fine detail I've got going on here."

"Well, it is nice, but it's only one level," she says.

You explain your logic, how it's the most important level. You talk about prisoners. Unicorn doesn't know why you would want to lock anyone up. But you don't back down.

Neither does she.

So you swipe your tail around and "accidental-ly" knock over her sandcastle. Then she accidentally stomps her hooves all over yours.

So much for that contest.

You try to remember the score but you're too an-noyed that she ruined your sandcastle dungeon (even though you ruined her sandcastle first, but who's keep-ing track?). Whatever.

You fly away.

The End

You turn to the big sink and you fill it with water and dish soap. You make sure there are so many bubbles that you can't see the water at all. Then you start washing. You wash one dish after another. So many dishes. The more you wash, the more fun it is. You sing a song, because even if you lose, having this much fun is like winning. When you are done with the dishes, you wash the glasses. Then the silverware. Then you wash all the big serving trays and stuff.

Once all the dishes are finished, you have a giant stack of drying dishes. It is a masterpiece.

You turn to Dragon. He's sitting there watching you. His stack of dirty dishes is still next to him. He hasn't washed a single one.

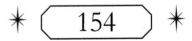

"You haven't washed a single one!" you say. Dragon is so lazy. You can't believe it. But once you get the trophy for winning this contest, you can always wash the rest. That would be a super fun way to spend the rest of the day.

"I guess you win," Dragon says. He doesn't seem to care.

The dishwasher carries in a giant gold trophy. Carved into it is the score of your victory.

Winner of this round: UNICORN

Overall score: UNICORN 4 – DRAGON 0

You open your mouth, ready to tell Dragon something like "Great contest" or "Nice try" or maybe even "Better luck next time." But before the words can leave your mouth Dragon grabs the trophy and flies away, out of the restaurant. He took your trophy! You can't believe it. You are seriously going to find that dragon and get your trophy back. But first you have a few more dishes to wash.

The End

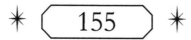

Sparkles are the answer to everything, no matter what the question is. You hurry to your costume closet and you pull out the sparkliest pants, shirt, hat, scarf, and sunglasses. They don't really go together, but they sure do sparkle. You put them on and hurry back to meet Dragon at the park.

You almost don't recognize him because he's painted his scales rainbow . . . just like your mane!

"I love your rainbows, Dragon," you say.

"Your sparkles aren't bad either," Dragon says.

"So tie?" you ask.

"Tie."

Winner of this round: <u>BOTH</u>

Overall score: <u>UNICORN 3 – DRAGON 3</u>

The End

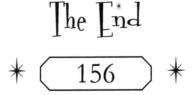

Unicorn's Perfect Milkshake Recipe
(Makes a perfect milkshake every time)

Get a large blender.
Place into the blender the following ingredients:

    1 gallon ice cream*
    ½ gallon whole milk
    Flavor**

Mix everything up until there are no chunks.
Enjoy!

* Stick with one fun flavor when it comes to ice cream. Fun flavors are things like butter cream pie, sunshine cookie, and sparkle pudding. Not fun flavors include smelly socks, week-old trash, or compost.
** Be creative when it comes to flavor. Rainbows, glitter, and happiness all make great milkshake flavors. Avoid unhappy flavors such as meanness, sadness, and liver.

Turn back to page 114.